Where's Molly?

Where's Molly?

Written and Illustrated by
Uli Waas

TRANSLATED BY
Rosemary Lanning

North-South Books
NEW YORK

Copyright © 1993 by Nord-Süd Verlag AG, Gossau Zürich, Switzerland
First published in Switzerland under the title *Molly ist weg*
English translation copyright © 1993 by Rosemary Lanning

First published in the United States, Great Britain, Canada,
Australia, and New Zealand in 1993 by North-South Books,
an imprint of Nord-Süd Verlag AG, Gossau Zürich, Switzerland.

Distributed in the United States by North-South Books Inc., New York.

Library of Congress Cataloging-in-Publication Data is available.
ISBN 1-55858-229-0 (TRADE BINDING)
ISBN 1-55858-230-4 (LIBRARY BINDING)

A CIP catalogue record for this book is available
from The British Library.

1 3 5 7 9 10 8 6 4 2
Printed in Belgium

It was New Year's Eve.
Lisa and Max were very excited.
"I can't wait for the party tonight!"
said Lisa.
"And the fireworks!" said Max.
"And we don't have to go to bed
until after midnight," said Lisa.
Molly, their dog, was excited too.

Molly would not have been excited
if she had known what fireworks were.
She was only a little dog
and she was scared of loud noises.
When there were thunderstorms,
Molly always stayed indoors,
hiding in her basket.

The party began at seven o'clock.
The table was spread
with good things to eat—
ham and salads and cakes and fruit.
The family who had just
moved in next door arrived first.
They had a little girl named Laura
and a boy named Nick.

When everyone had finished eating,
the children played under the table.

Then they played catch
with a tennis ball.
Molly ran back and forth
across the room, chasing the ball.
Molly loved all the games,
but soon she got tired
and curled up on
some pillows to rest.
The children cuddled her
and gave her treats.

When it was nearly midnight,
everyone went into the sitting room.
Dad looked at his watch and counted:
"Three, two, one . . . midnight!"
Everyone shouted "Happy New Year!"
Church bells rang, and outside
the window, rockets whizzed and banged.
The sky was lit up by flashes of red,
yellow, and green.
Molly crept away to her basket
and covered her ears with her paws.

The children ran into the garden,
and Dad came out to light some rockets.
The first rocket shot up into the sky.
Bang! Blue and white stars burst from it
and floated down over the garden.
It was so pretty.

The children stood and stared.
They forgot that they had left
the door open.
Suddenly Molly dashed through
the open door and ran across the garden.
"Molly!" yelled Lisa.
"Molly! Stop! Come back!" shouted Max.
But it was too late. Molly was gone.

Max and Lisa ran after the little dog.
But Molly was too fast
and too frightened,
and they could not catch her

"Come back, children,"
said their mother. "Let's try to think
where Molly would go
to get away from the fireworks."
They looked in every dark, quiet corner
along the street—in doorways,
in garages, and under bushes—
but they did not find Molly.
The fireworks had stopped
and there was silence all around.
Max heard a rustle.
"Molly?" he whispered.
But it was only a mouse.

They looked and looked,
but still they did not find Molly.
It was very late. Max was so tired
that Mother had to put him to bed.
All the party guests went home.
Dad said he would take the car
and go on looking for Molly.
"Do you want to come with me, Lisa?"
he asked. Lisa nodded.

They drove slowly along the main road
and down the narrow back streets,
but they did not see any dogs at all.
It was three o'clock in the morning
when they got back home.

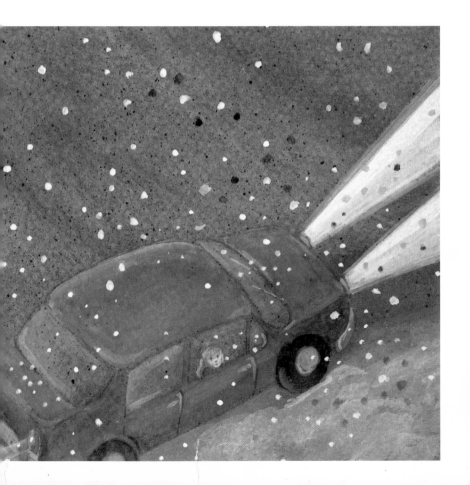

Dad went sadly into the garden
to pick up all the unused rockets.
"There is nothing more we can do
until tomorrow morning," he said.
Lisa was crying.
Her mother hugged her.

"Don't cry," she said. "I'm sure someone
has found Molly and she is safe.
Now you need some sleep."

The next morning at breakfast
everyone was sad and worried.
No one felt very hungry.
It was not a happy New Year.
"Do you think Molly has fallen
in the river and drowned?" said Max.
"No," said Mother, "dogs can swim."

"But the river is so cold," said Lisa.
"She would be frozen."
Dad got up from the table.
"I'm going to call
the animal shelter," he said.
"Someone may have found Molly
and taken her there."
"Is she there?" asked Mother
when Dad put down the phone.
"No," he said, "but they will let us know
if someone brings her in.
Come on, Max, let's go and have
another look for her."
Lisa and her mother stayed behind.
Five minutes later
the telephone rang.
It was the
animal shelter!

Someone had just brought in a little dog.

It might be Molly!

Lisa and her mother danced with joy.

An hour later Dad and Max came home.
They looked very sad.

Lisa ran outside to tell them
the good news.
Then Lisa and her mother ran
to put their coats on, and they all
raced out to the car.

They were still worried as they drove
to the animal shelter.
What if it wasn't Molly?
When they arrived, they could hear
lots of dogs barking.
"That's Molly!" cried Max, waving
his hat in the air. "I know her bark."
"I hope you're right," said Mother.

In the animal shelter there was
a pen full of dogs—

big ones and small ones, fluffy ones
and spotted ones. But where was Molly?

"Some of these dogs
ran away from home," said the woman
in charge of the shelter. "And some
were not wanted by their owners."
Suddenly a little dog
ran to the front of the pen.
It was Molly!
She jumped up at the wire fence
and wagged her tail.

At last the door of the pen was opened.
Molly ran out and licked Max's face.

Lisa looked at the other dogs.
"I wish we could take them all home,"
she said sadly.
"We can't do that," said Dad,
"but we can give some money
to help feed them."

"Who brought our little dog here?"
asked Mother.

"Someone called Emily Button,"
said the woman who ran the shelter.
"I wrote down her address.
Here it is: Seventeen Park Street."
They wondered what Emily Button
was like. Max thought she sounded like
somebody's grandmother.

On the way home both Max and Lisa
wanted to hold Molly.
Molly did not mind whose lap she sat on.
She was just glad to be back
with her family.

When they got home,
they gave Molly a big bone
and watched her chew it.
They were so happy to have her back.
"Now we must go and thank
old Miss Button," said Mother.
"Let's buy her some flowers
and take Molly with us."

Max rang Miss Button's doorbell.
The door was opened by a young woman
with a huge black and brown dog.

She was not a grandmother at all!
Emily Button looked at Molly and said,
"Look who's come to see us, Nero."
Lisa gave her the flowers
and asked how she had found Molly.
"Come in, and I will tell you
all about it," said Emily.

Miss Button told them
that she had gone for a walk
with a friend late on New Year's Eve.
Suddenly they heard a little whimper
and looked up. There was Molly
on top of a wall. A firework banged,
and Molly jumped down into Emily's
arms. Emily took the little dog home.
When they got home, Molly ran straight
to Nero's food dish. The big dog
didn't mind at all. He just waited
until she had finished and then ate
what was left. Then the two dogs
had fun playing together.

In the morning Emily took Molly
to the animal shelter.
"I really wanted to keep her," she said,
"but I knew her family
would want her back."
"Thank you so much," said Dad.
He looked down. Molly was gone again!
"I think I know where to find her,"
said Emily, and she went into
the kitchen.
There was Molly with her front paws
in Nero's food dish.

Molly gobbled Nero's food,
but he didn't seem to mind.
"It's time we took her home,"
said Mother.

That evening Max and Lisa
took Molly for a walk.
"From now on, when there are fireworks,
we will keep you safe indoors," said Lisa.
"Yes," said Max. "We don't want you
to run away ever again."
As soon as Max said "run," Molly started
to scamper across the snow.
Max and Lisa trotted along behind her,
shouting, "Happy New Year!"

About the Author/Illustrator

Uli Waas was born in 1949 in Donauwörth in Bavaria, which is in southern Germany. She studied art and design at the Art Academy in Munich. Uli has been a children's book illustrator for quite a few years now. She loves to draw children, mice, bears, and, of course, the family dog, Jeany, who is the model for Molly in this story. Jeany is a Jack Russell terrier. She is a lively little dog who keeps the family on its toes and provides perfect material for stories.

**Little Polar Bear
and the Brave Little Hare**
by Hans de Beer

•

Rinaldo, the Sly Fox
by Ursel Scheffler
illustrated by Iskender Gider

The Return of Rinaldo, the Sly Fox
by Ursel Scheffler
illustrated by Iskender Gider

•

Loretta and the Little Fairy
by Gerda Marie Scheidl
illustrated by Christa Unzner-Fischer